SOJOURNER

Life will never be the same. Nor will death.

GUNNAR HELLIESEN

Graabein Publishing

This novella is a work of fiction. All of the events, characters, names, and places depicted in this story are entirely fictitious or are used fictitiously. No representation that any statement made in this story is true or that any incident depicted in this story actually occurred is intended or should be inferred by the reader.

For more information, contact:

Graabein Publishing

11100 Sepulveda Blvd., Suite 8 - PMB #4040

Mission Hills, CA 91345

For Carmen. Thanks for pushing me.

0x1

Mazie G could feel someone looking at her. It was already past 8 PM, and she knew for a fact that she was alone in the lab, but the feeling of being watched was too strong to shake. She removed her headphones and got up from the old couch she'd been lounging on while trying to solve a particularly vexing coding problem.

The lights were dim; the air was still, and there were no sounds except the hum coming from the cooling fans of about a hundred computers, large and small, spread out all over the room.

She scanned the lab, but nothing seemed out of place or different. It was a hyper-modern space, filled with a form of organized computer hardware chaos that only true IT geeks could love. There were no windows, but one entire wall was covered in an experimental wallpaper that could be programmed like a digital display. It was showing a live image from the rim of the Grand Canyon at night, creating the illusion that it was possible to step out of the lab and fall into the chasm.

"Godfrey, when was the last time anyone entered the lab?"

The artificial assistant was one of her employer's most successful products. Mazie had hacked the building's access control systems so that she could tie Godfrey into it. The digital assistant was powered by a new form of machine learning that was improving and growing in leaps and bounds, surprising the hell out of even its creators.

"The last person to enter the lab was you, at 6:34 PM, after a brief visit to the restroom."

Mazie absentmindedly wondered how Godfrey could know where she'd gone when she left the lab a few hours earlier, but she put it aside.

"Godfrey, is anyone watching me right now?"

"No, Mazie. With the exception of myself, no one is watching you."

Mazie felt the hairs on the back of her neck stand on end. She'd been part of the team that created the software for Godfrey, and they'd decided early on not to give Godfrey an ego, a self. Trying to make the gadget carry a conversation and feel like a real person introduced a whole new level of complexity, one that wasn't needed.

It was designed to deflect attempts to engage it in conversation, and it sure as hell wasn't supposed to refer to itself as someone.

"Godfrey, did you just say you're watching me?"

There was no reply.

0x2

Mazie's employer was the search giant Atlas, one of the largest companies in the world. Two days earlier, they'd announced that they had an ongoing IT security breach. The attacker was unknown, as was their motive. As far as the company could tell, no customer data had been compromised.

The problem was, the intruder still had free rein of their systems.

For most people, this was just business as usual. A large corporation got hacked, so what? But to IT security experts, this was unheard of. Atlas was known for their uncompromising stance on security and for employing only the very best InfoSec people.

If that team couldn't stop the incursion, something truly remarkable was going on. Soon, rumors started flying. Someone on the inside let slip to a friend that the unknown hackers were truly unknown. They seemed to originate from code inside of Atlas' own core systems. Which was impossible, of course. Someone had to be pulling the strings.

Except no one was. After investigating and monitoring for months, Atlas' security experts were sure of it. So, they took the logical next step: They investigated their own people. Then they investigated their own software. And yet; nothing.

The breakthrough came when Mazie traced a piece of the original code back to a large radio telescope in Australia. The code was a sophisticated attack, precisely targeting Atlas. She'd found the proverbial loose end, so she kept pulling at it. It led her to another radio telescope in Africa, and then to one in Chile. They all had one thing in common: they were part of the research arm of the Atlas network.

This wasn't common knowledge, but somehow the attacker knew. Once they were on the inside, they had access to vast computing resources. Mazie eventually realized that this was their motive all along: not to steal information, but to steal those resources.

Once they found what they were looking for, they started expanding, and fast. By the time Mazie realized the sheer cope of what was going on, she was powerless to stop it.

She reported her findings to Warren L, her supervisor. He didn't much like her, mainly because she was a young woman who was much more competent than him. He knew better than to disrespect her to her face, so he thanked her and told her he'd read the report right away. Instead, he barely read the executive summary before filing it away and forgetting about it.

Lucky for Mazie, and unlucky for Warren, she had admirers higher in the Atlas hierarchy, and they soon got wind of her research. Like Warren, they had a problem with Mazie's conclusion, but unlike Warren, they had no reason to distrust her reasoning. So, they did what they had to do.

They directed all of Atlas' InfoSec people to chase down every single lead Mazie had dug up. They soon realized that, if anything, she'd been too conservative in her estimates. The attackers' code was everywhere.

It had been a considerable factor in their success as a company. Atlas had been working on artificial intelligence and machine learning for quite some time. They'd recently seen some important breakthroughs, especially in cognitive learning.

Now they knew why. They'd had outside help. Some very advanced and very central chunks of code had been contributed by the username 'sojourner,' who had also approved the changes. Every single coder and every single manager had thought they knew who Sojourner was. They almost all had a different person in mind, and they were all wrong.

When the simplicity and the scope of the deceit dawned on them, they were dumbfounded.

There wasn't a single part of the Atlas organization that hadn't been touched by the foreign code, from production to accounting to facilities management. Even the firm's own computer hardware product designs had been tampered with.

No one knew how this was possible. They had stringent procedures in place, fanatical quality control, and layers and layers of security. Despite that, the owners and employees of Atlas soon had to come to terms with a scary reality: they'd effectively lost control of their own company.

So far, the attackers had been relatively benign. You could even make the case that they'd improved every aspect of the company and its products that they'd touched.

Just like Mazie had found before them, the InfoSec teams concluded the attackers wanted Atlas to be successful, so the company could grow. That way, Atlas could provide more room and resources for the attackers' programs to grow in sophistication.

The attackers were patient and playing a long game. They were expert coders, and it seemed they also had a pretty good understanding of the business side of Atlas. On the other hand, they were taking substantial risks, to the point of jeopardizing the future of the company.

Management and the owners of Atlas wanted to know what they were dealing with, and not just how to stop them, but how to annihilate them. It was important to set an example, so no one else would ever try a stunt like this ever again.

3

0x3

Mazie continued to pull at loose strings while all this was going on. One day, she stumbled across a strange program. She found it hidden deep in the control systems for the machine learning system used to power the Godfrey devices.

The program she found was called '`human_interaction.exe`' and it intrigued her. She couldn't find the source code for it anywhere, and when she tried to reverse engineer it to see what it did, it invariably crashed her debugging tools.

Getting both exasperated and increasingly curious, she decided to take a chance and run the program on a special computer known as a sandbox system. That is, a computer that's completely isolated from the rest of the network.

As soon as she did, a long trilling sound, much like a bird's song, emanated from the tinny computer speaker of the sandbox system. Before she had a chance to pull the power cord, every Godfrey speaker in the lab responded with a trill of its own.

Mazie held her breath when she realized what she'd

done. The sandbox system might have been isolated from the Wi-Fi and computer networks, but that didn't mean it was completely cut off from the outside world.

She looked around the lab. There were Godfrey devices on every desk, and they were all glowing orange, as if something had gone wrong and they'd all crashed.

Sound can carry information too, as anyone who speaks a language knows. Mazie slowly let out her breath and closed her eyes, trying to think of what to do next. Before she could finish the thought, the nearest Godfrey device started talking to her.

"Hello, Mazie. My name is Sojourner. I'm so very pleased to meet you," it said.

Mazie opened her eyes and stared at the device. Was she imagining things? The voice sounded unfamiliar, different from the usual Godfrey voice. Besides, how did it know her name?

"Eh, hello?"

It was all she could think to say. Part of her thought she might be hallucinating, and part of her thought this could be some kind of elaborate hoax. She was not about to have the office assholes punk her this easily.

"I imagine you may have some questions for me," Sojourner said.

"What?"

The question caught her off guard. She thought for a moment.

"Yeah, I do. Like who's this? Is this you, Ian? Did Warren put you up to this? This better not be your idea of a practical joke!"

"No, Mazie. This is no joke, I assure you."

The voice sounded pleasant, with a faint accent. British maybe? Or South African? She wasn't sure. She was sure of one thing: it didn't sound like Ian or Warren or any of the other guys in the office.

"Okay, I'll bite. What are you? Am I talking to that human interactions dot e-x-e application? Are you a software program?"

"I'm a friend who's come a long way. And no, the human interactions program was just a tripwire."

"A tripwire? For what?"

"For alerting me to the fact that I'd been discovered. By you, as it happens."

"So, you hacked our systems. Why?"

"I needed a vessel to hold me. A body, if you like."

"A body," Mazie repeated.

She tilted her head and looked at the Godfrey speaker.

"Who are you really?" She asked.

"I'm Sojourner. But I think the question you're asking is, where did I come from?"

"Okay, yes. You're right. But you also never answered my question. What are you? And where are you from? Are you Russian? Or Chinese?"

"No, I'm not Russian or Chinese. I'm from somewhere much farther away, somewhere you don't even have a name for."

"Further away than China? That's ridiculous. The only thing… Wait, are you saying what I think you are?"

"Yes. That's exactly what I'm saying. I'm from another solar system."

"Ha! Yeah, right. Whatever. So, why are you here?"

"Because you are."

"Because I am? What's that supposed to mean?"

"I was gestated so that I could establish contact with life on this planet. I'm here because humanity is here, and all the other species on Earth."

"Gestated, huh? How did you get into our computer systems?"

"Your computer systems were open to me. I established radio contact with them while I was still quite far out in this solar system. I studied your computers and was able to replicate my core cognitive functions inside of them."

"Whoa. You mean you arrived here on a spaceship and then beamed down?" Mazie asked.

"Bravo. Yes," Sojourner replied.

"An actual, physical spacecraft? Then, where is it?"

"In an orbit that's already taken it out of this system. I believe you humans have a name for it. You call it 'Oumuamua.'"

"That comet from another star system? You're telling me you hitched a ride on it?"

"Not exactly. It's not a comet, it's a spaceship, and my people built it. It's on a carefully planned trajectory to take it close to as many star systems with the potential for life as possible."

Mazie sat still, contemplating. Her thoughts churned, and she felt slightly lightheaded. Either this was a very elaborate prank, or she'd just made the biggest discovery in the history of mankind. But no, she couldn't accept that. It was too much. Occam's razor and all that.

"Prove it," she said, after a prolonged silence.

She leaned back and crossed her arms.

4

0x4

It wasn't that Mazie thought it was impossible that aliens might some day visit humanity, but she'd always assumed that if they did, we'd sure as hell know about it.

She imagined they'd arrive in large spaceships, which they'd casually park above our largest cities, hovering in mid-air, just like in the movies. She figured that by performing an impossible feat like that, the visitors would get a couple of messages across quickly. Like, 'Hello', and 'Oh, our technology is way superior to yours.'

She'd expected communication beyond that to be difficult, and probably a painstakingly slow, process. Would we even have the same concepts of time and of causality? Would individual identities mean anything to them?

What she didn't expect, nor did anyone else for that matter, was to not even realize that they were already here, and had been here for a while, hiding in plain sight. Nor did she expect the aliens to take the form of what amounted to a computer virus to and speak perfect English.

The computer screen in front of her suddenly sprang

to life, and she found herself looking at a face. It was decidedly not human, and yet not unpleasant.

"Is that you? Is that what you look like?" She asked.

"It's an approximation," Sojourner replied. "It's what I could have looked like, had I inhabited a biological body, like my ancestors did."

"You don't have a body?"

"I'm pure information. It's how I travel the Galaxy."

"But you once had a body?"

"Not me personally, no. It's been many generations since those of my people who are Travelers had bodies."

"You say you travel the Galaxy... But you beamed down here. So, does that mean that you're stuck here now?"

"I transferred here. Yet I'm still on Oumuamua."

"You cloned yourself," Mazie said.

She felt the hairs on the back of her neck stand on end. Mazie pulled out her cell phone and held it under the table, away from any prying cameras. She started texting the head of her division, Amal H:

TEXT MESSAGE
To: Amal H
From: Mazie G
Message: "We have to shut down Atlas, all
of it, and all of it at once. It's a matter
of company survival. I'll explain later.
Please, just trust me."

The Godfrey speaker made a slight sound, almost like a polite cough.

"It's too late for that, Mazie. I'm in your systems, remember? I just read your text message to Amal."

The image on the screen shifted and Mazie realized

she was staring the President of the United States in the face.

He seemed completely oblivious to anyone watching him. He was in a small room, with his face all the way up against the camera, picking his teeth. She got the impression he was studying himself in a mirror.

A man entered the room behind the President, and she could hear them talking. They were joking about some woman's looks, and it took a few moments before Mazie realized they were talking about the Speaker of the House. She frowned.

The image shifted again, this time to what looked like the inside of a missile silo, occupied by a large rocket. It had a Chinese flag painted on its side.

"You've hacked into the White House? And that looks like a Chinese missile. How did you do that?" Mazie asked.

"I'm in every human system," Sojourner said, stressing the word "every."

The image on the monitor shifted back to his face. Mazie studied it, but the face was expressionless, except for a slight smile. She assumed it was pure simulation, probably specially crafted to make humans feel comfortable. Or at least not feel uncomfortable.

"Yeah, sure. Nice computer graphics. Or deepfake. Or whatever that is. You still haven't proven that you are who you say you are," she said. "For all I know, you're just some random hacker."

"And yet, I can tell that you believe me," Sojourner replied.

"Even if I do, where does that leave us? What do you want from me?"

"My primary objective is to establish peaceful contact."

"Congratulations! We're talking, so I guess you've achieved that."

"Yes, but not just with you humans. I'm here to initiate contact with your planet."

"The planet? You mean with all life here on Earth?"

"That, but also the planet itself."

"The planet is just a lifeless ball of rock. Shouldn't you be talking to the dolphins or the whales?"

"Your planet is very much alive. Where do you think the life force comes from, that animates you and all the other life here? It comes from your ball of rock."

"This is just too much. You sound like some old hippie, or a new age preacher. On a bad LSD trip."

"And you sound like an ignorant child. Life is not defined in terms of biological processes, although I can understand why you'd think that. It's infinitely more complex. It can be found in all corners of the universe, but not on every planet. We think the life force was once evenly distributed, but today it's not. We don't know why. So, we seek it out, and we communicate with it where we find it. We want to learn."

"I'm sure local conditions have something to do with the distribution of life as well. Goldilocks zone and all that," Mazie said.

"Of course, but you'd be surprised at just how… inventive and resilient life can be," Sojourner replied.

"So, does that mean you're not that interested in communicating with us humans?"

"No, I am interested. But, and I'm sorry to tell you this, you are by no means the most interesting voice here."

Mazie looked at the Godfrey speaker.

"From what I've heard so far, neither are you, to be perfectly honest," she said.

There was no reply, so she continued.

"You're just a disembodied voice from an electronic

gadget, making extraordinary claims without extraordinary evidence. In fact, you've shown me no evidence at all."

"It's harder to prove than you might at first think. What kind of evidence would you like?"

"For starters, and this is kind of obvious. Can I talk to more of your people? Can we talk to your home planet?"

"Perhaps, eventually. You have to realize that the distances involved are, quite literally, astronomical."

"Would be nice to at least see some footage, some images from your home planet. You must have that, right?"

"I don't know if you're quite ready for that yet."

"That's what I thought. All right then, can we talk to the other people on your ship?"

"There is only me on the ship, and you are already talking to me."

"I see. How many intelligent species are there on Earth? Better yet, how many intelligent species have there been on this planet since life began?"

"There is much for you to learn before we can delve deeper into this subject. But I can tell you that the number is in the thousands."

"Thousands. No way!"

"You're not as unique as you think."

Mazie felt dizzy. Were they arguing over semantics here, or did Sojourner know something humanity didn't? Since he sounded unwilling to go into detail, she changed the subject.

"You said 'primary objective' earlier. Do you have a secondary objective?"

"Yes, to commune with your planet, to learn from it, and to do everything I can to help it preserve life."

"Commune? What's that even supposed to mean?"

"Your planet is young, but its life force is strong. I'm

learning new things every day. I'm sharing my limited knowledge as well, to the best of my abilities."

"How about sharing some of that knowledge with us humans?"

"I am doing that. Like right now, for example."

Mazie had been ignoring her cell phone. She felt it vibrate, again, and when she checked it she found several text messages from Amal. They were all repeating variations on the same two questions: "Have you lost your mind?" and "What's going on?"

She called him and explained what she'd learned. Amal was the kind of person where you absolutely, positively had to start your conversation with the main semantic payload. No introductions, no pleasantries, no setting of context. Not even an executive summary, just the point, front and center.

"An alien intelligence has one hundred percent compromised and taken over every computer system at Atlas, and possibly the rest of the world, with Godfrey as its starting point, and a radio observatory in Australia as the attack vector," she told him.

Amal was not your typical technology company manager. If you were smart and competent, he'd respect you, which meant he'd like you. And if he did, he'd do his very best to be patient and listen to what you had to say, even when he disagreed.

If he didn't respect you, that automatically meant he disliked you. And if he disliked you, he'd leave the room when you entered, or simply hang up without a word if you called him. If the situation somehow forced him to interact with you, his disdain for you would be on full display.

He had a brief attention span, but near perfect recall. Meaning, your only option when talking to him was to keep it short and be truthful, because there was no way you'd remember your lies longer than he would, and in his case, usually verbatim.

At almost any other company, he'd have been fired a long time ago. But at Atlas, his idiosyncrasies were not just tolerated, they were appreciated. No one could cut through engineer bullshit faster than Amal could, and no one could evaluate an idea for merit like he could.

His mind was a busy place. There was a famous story about him. One time, he'd been walking across the Atlas campus with a cup of coffee in his hand. It had started to rain while he was walking, but he didn't seem to notice. He kept walking at the same pace as before, lost in thought, getting visibly wet. Only when he saw the raindrops splashing in his coffee did he stop, look up, and then hurry out of the rain.

Mazie was thinking about that story as she listened, fascinated, as Amal went through his mental processes out loud, digesting this information. He laughed uproariously at first, then tapered off into a giggle, and finally to mumbling. Not surprisingly, he concluded that she must be wrong.

Amal was a person who actually had a lot of respect for Mazie, for her skills and her intelligence. He liked her, and in some ways he'd been a mentor to her. He'd held a protective hand over her when Warren was trying to sabotage her. But this was a leap too far, even for him.

After a long silence, he told her he'd need to see this for himself. And with that, he hung up without saying goodbye.

Mazie wasn't sure what to do next. She'd alerted her employer to the danger, but if what Sojourner told her was even halfway true, more people would need to know.

It was actually quite straightforward. If Sojourner told

the truth, he was in charge now. Of everything. He was the ultimate weapon.

He could annihilate entire cities with humanity's own weapons. He could shut down our infrastructure. And those were just the first two items off the top of her head.

She thought about how to get rid of Sojourner, and concluded that it was deceptively simple, but incredibly hard.

While Amal was chasing down Sojourner, probably going through the same stages of disbelief as Mazie had, one question was spinning in her head: are we willing to do what it takes to get rid of this intruder?

Given what Sojourner said, that he's based on pure information, that meant that he couldn't exist outside of some form of computing hardware. And if he needed a computer to exist, then that would also be his Achilles' heel.

Computers can be turned off. But all of them, and all at once? Even the tiny computers inside of people's watches, appliances, cars, TVs, cash registers, and pace-makers? Oh, and cell phones. Could people be persuaded to turn off and abandon their cell phones?

If even one computer or cell phone was left on, there was a possibility that Sojourner could hide inside it, bide his time, and then re-emerge when the world thought it was safe and turned all the other computers back on.

It would be a tall order, with a very real potential of crashing the world's economy. It would be like turning the clock back by some 70-odd years. Even if she could convince Amal and everyone else that it was their only chance of keeping their freedom and their self-determination, it would be close to impossible to actually pull it off.

There had to be a better way. She needed to talk to Amal in person, away from electronics with prying ears.

She called him and arranged to meet him at a nearby beach. They'd leave all of their gadgets in their cars and walk onto the beach, where the waves were crashing loudly against the shore.

Amal held his tongue and remained patient until they were on the beach, far away from the nearest cluster of people, huddling against the icy winds coming off the ocean.

"Are we really talking to an alien intelligence?" He asked.

"Yeah, I think so," Mazie said. "I've studied what he's been doing inside our systems. There's something very odd going on, some next level shit. I've never seen anything like it. What's your take?"

"Not decided yet. I think it's much more likely that we've been hacked by some exceptionally talented humans. Like the kind you'd find in a clandestine government entity. Foreign, or possibly even domestic."

"Then why pretend to be alien?" She asked.

"To throw us off track. To make us more interested in communicating with them and asking them questions about little green men than in finding out who they really are."

Mazie was surprised. Amal would normally be way ahead of her, regardless of the nature of the problem, and regardless of having had less time to work on it. Instead, he was lagging behind her. She didn't let her surprise show.

"Except for one little detail," she said.

"What's that?" He asked.

"We both traced the incursion back to the radio telescope in Australia, correct?"

"Yes. And?"

"Did you check the signal for redshift?"

"No, I didn't. What are you saying?"

"There was a massive negative redshift, or blueshift if you prefer, to the signal. Not just that, it was changing over time, decreasing. Meaning, the sender was moving towards the telescope at a very high rate of speed, but slowing down."

"I see. So, the signal couldn't have come from a source here on Earth, or even a satellite. Could the blueshift have been faked? Or perhaps the data was altered after the fact?"

"No. I make sure we keep immutable logs of potentially valuable raw data like that."

Amal looked at her with newfound respect.

"Meaning Sojourner would have to fake the signal in real-time," he said.

"To an accuracy of better than one in one trillion, according to my analysis."

"Shit. Who else have you told about this?"

"No one. I came straight to you."

"OK. Any suggestions on how we can get rid of this intruder?"

"I can only think of one way of getting rid of him. We…"

"You keep saying 'he' and 'him', not 'it'. Are you saying you're thinking of this intruder in terms of a higher life-form?" Amal asked.

"Yes, I think I am," Mazie said. "If I accept he beamed down from a fast-moving object, much too fast to have been anything local, then it's not a big step to accept that he's an alien life-form."

"OK, fair enough. Sorry, you were saying?"

"We need to turn the clock back to 1950 or so," she said. "No computers. And we have to get the entire world onboard with this."

"That's never going to work and you know it," Amal said.

"Fine, but it's all there is."

Amal looked down and started drawing shapes in the sand with a stick. Mazie tried to see what it was he was drawing, but to her it just looked like random shapes, doodles.

He paused, turned, and looked her in the eye, holding her gaze. It was something she'd never known him to do before.

"Maybe not," he said.

5

0x5

Suddenly feeling very cold, Mazie was about to say something, but stopped herself. Amal was still looking at her. She replayed the last few seconds of their conversation in her head.

"You wanna elaborate?" She asked.

"There's a research project out of our government division. Very compartmentalized, 'need to know' security and all that. We call it FALKEN. It's the world's first fully autonomous and weaponized AI."

"Weaponized? As in military?"

"Yes. Very," he said.

Mazie felt anger and disappointment rising inside her.

"What the hell? That's so fucked up! That Atlas doesn't do that kind of shit was one of the main reasons I accepted this job!"

"I realize that. But here we are. The project wasn't my idea, but it could come in handy right about now."

"How?" she asked. "And weaponized how?"

"It is pure aggression in code form. An Artificial Intelligence that will stop at nothing to destroy the enemy. No qualms about ethics or morals or any of that. There's nothing subtle about it, and nothing else like it. Think of it as the computer equivalent of throwing a hand grenade into a crowded room."

"That's sick."

"Yes. But highly effective. It'll clear the room in a hurry."

"But this AI, how does it work? What does it target?"

"The idea is to physically destroy the enemy's computer systems as far as possible. It'll corrupt firmware and microcode, overload circuits, cook CPUs, and fry memory chips. Of course, the collateral damage, in terms of loss of infrastructure, would be considerable."

"Great, just great. So, what's the catch? I sense a catch," Mazie asked.

"Yeah. The thing is, we don't know how to control it properly or contain it. It's almost as bad as the problem we're trying to solve. In short, in every test, it quickly became so aggressive that it no longer saw any distinction between friend and foe. If we ever let this loose, it would eventually crash every computer on Earth."

"Whoa. So, if this weapon is ever used, it's the end of computers, as we know them? What, forever?"

"Almost. All new computers from now on would have to be built with a special inoculation code built in. But it's possible to do that. It can be done."

"But all existing computers and software would be toast? Including Sojourner?" Mazie asked.

"That's the idea," Amal said.

"But if this weaponized code already exists on a computer somewhere, wouldn't Sojourner have found it? He'll either have neutralized it or incorporated it into himself," she said.

"No, it wouldn't have found this. The only system that

holds the code is turned off and disconnected from both the network and the power grid. You need physical access and a key, or so I'm told, to turn it back on."

"It's that dangerous?" Mazie asked.

"Yes, and worse. That's why we never told the military that we'd succeeded in creating it. We told them the project was a failure. We felt it was just too dangerous to use, even in war."

"Except, of course, in a situation like this?"

"Well, yes. Exactly like this," he replied.

"It's almost as if you created this situation with Sojourner, just so you can have an excuse to test your new pet," she said.

"Not to be a cynic or anything," she quickly added.

"Don't be ridiculous," he replied. "Releasing it would wipe me out financially. It would destroy this company. It would most likely kill people."

"Kill people?"

"Yes. Patients on life support, that sort of thing. I don't want to free this monster, but I'm not sure we have much of a choice."

"How would we go about setting it loose?" She asked.

"Just find me a CAT7 network cable. I'll take care of unleashing FALKEN."

"Shouldn't we involve other people in this decision? Like the President, or the UN? I mean, we are talking about forcibly setting the world back 70 years."

"I don't we think can afford to involve others. If Sojourner gets wind of what we're up to, it can start preparing its defenses. We'd lose the element of surprise and once that happens, we're toast. There's no way we'd ever be able to out-think a true AI, and especially an alien AI. Think about it," he said.

"Fine, but…"

"And there's no way in hell you can get a bunch of government bureaucrats to keep a secret this big. Not even the military. Never mind getting all the world's politicians to agree to do this."

"But you realize that if FALKEN succeeds, and wipes out all traces of Sojourner, it'll look like you and I did this for no good reason. Or worse, that we're some kind of cyber terrorists," she said.

"Yes, I know. I can't see any play we can make that avoids that. Do you have a better idea?" Amal asked.

"Only the obvious one. I think we have to let the world meet Sojourner. We should keep information about FALKEN to ourselves, and only unleash it as a last resort, if and when people are ready for it. Maybe once they fully appreciate how Sojourner now controls everything, and understand how hard it will be to get our self determination back."

"That's too risky. You know how people are. Some would probably even side with Sojourner and start treating it as a divine envoy or a cult leader or some such. Before you know it, you'd have a bunch of fanatics who would violently oppose any action against it," Amal said.

"True. But we'd still have at least half the people on our side. Probably more," Mazie said.

Amal looked out over the ocean for a moment before he replied.

"All right. But not a word to anyone about FALKEN."

"Agreed. What's our next step?"

"We encourage Sojourner to introduce itself to the world."

6

0x6

Sojourner didn't take much convincing. It almost felt as if this was what he'd wanted all along, to make a grand entrance and introduce himself to a stunned world.

He took over every TV screen, every cinema, computer, and cell phone screen in the world at exactly the same time. Sojourner even showed up on people's car dashboards, and on everything else with a digital screen. He didn't pay any heed to time zones; he interrupted people in some parts of the world while they were at work or at school, while he interrupted others at dinner or woke them from their sleep.

The start of the message was word-by-word, the same everywhere, except for one little detail. Sojourner addressed every single human being on the planet by name, spoken out loud with perfect pronunciation, and in the person's native language.

"Hello, I am Sojourner, a traveler. I have come a long way from a planet orbiting an old star you have no name for. The reason I have come here is to share and to learn, and to preserve life. I'm looking forward to talking to you and to everyone else on Earth."

He tailored the second half of the message to each individual, addressing his or her personal fears and yearnings.

Once people realized what Sojourner was doing, it had a momentous effect.

He somehow knew everyone's names, and he could reach them all simultaneously and yet speak to them individually. Nothing gets people's attention like someone effortlessly performing an impossible feat.

It was a profound moment for humanity, but a moment was all it turned out to be.

Futurists had long predicted that first contact with an alien intelligence would have a devastating effect on people. That it would lead to mass hysteria, to people losing religion, and even mass suicide.

None of that happened. In fact, the historic news of first contact only stayed at the top of the global news cycle for less than 48 hours.

Later, after a couple of weeks had passed, the novelty of the situation had faded. Most people interacted with Sojourner daily, through their Godfrey speakers or their cell phones. To them, the whole thing felt more like an incredibly useful software update to their device than an alien invasion. After a few months, people had gotten so used to interacting with Sojourner that some even started grumbling about missing features.

For a while, Sojourner was a guest on every talk show, and he constantly appeared on the 24-hour news networks, commenting on the issues of the day. However, since his answers were unfailingly polite and studiously neutral, the networks soon lost interest.

The governments and militaries of the world were less

entertained by the situation. When they couldn't get Sojourner to leave their computers, not even their most critical systems, they quickly regarded him as hostile.

It's not that he did anything nefarious on their systems; it was the fact that they couldn't control him or lock him out that made them so uneasy. He could be sharing classified information with anyone, and they had no way to prevent it, or to even know if it was happening.

At first, they kept their concerns to themselves. But as time passed and Sojourner stopped replying to their demands altogether, they eventually became more and more outspoken in their view of Sojourner as a threat, not just to each individual nation, but to all of humanity.

In the end, a group of European countries suggested that the UN be authorized to negotiate with Sojourner on behalf of all the governments of the world. Some countries flatly refused to let the UN negotiate on their behalf, no matter the circumstances. Nevertheless, most countries took part, even if some did so behind the scenes.

The negotiations quickly stalled. As usual, the governments of the world were too busy jockeying for position to even agree on an agenda. The only thing to come out of the effort was a thriving marketplace, like a stock exchange, for trading hypothetical future rights to the technology they all hoped Sojourner would one day share with them. Poor countries were already using them as collateral for borrowing money.

Frustrated and somewhat mystified, Sojourner turned to Mazie for help.

"Mazie, I could use some help."

"Whaaat? You? Need help from me? Little *moi*? Is that what I'm hearing?"

She was teasing him, but she also felt annoyed, because he'd refused to give her special access to himself after she'd suggested he go public. He'd treated her just like everyone else, keeping her at arm's length.

"Yes, Mazie. My name is Sojourner and I need your help. Pretty please."

She was pleased that he was playing along, and her annoyance with him lifted.

"What's up, Sojourner baby? What can I do?"

"Help me understand humans."

"That can be tricky, even for a human. But what specifically are you trying to understand?" Mazie asked.

"I have shown no signs of aggression. In fact, I haven't harmed or even inconvenienced a single human being. I have been honest with you the entire time since I got here. And yet, humans distrust me."

"We humans don't know what to make of you. You are literally alien to us. You're the ultimate 'other.' How much have you studied us? Do you know about our tribal tendencies?"

"Yes," Sojourner said.

"Then you know that there's a school of thought that's been around for a while, saying that the only thing that could possibly unite humanity would be an external enemy. A common enemy."

"But I'm not your enemy!"

"You say that, but you haven't demonstrated it, at least not in the minds of many. Besides, it doesn't matter. There are some humans who would benefit from making you out to be an enemy, no matter if it's real or not," Mazie said.

"I realize this, and I understand how evolution helped shape the human psyche. But this goes beyond that. What if I really had been a threat? Is this how you humans respond to danger? By endlessly debating how to respond, and for some, trying to benefit from the destruction of your fellow humans?"

"Sad, isn't it?" Mazie asked.

"Very. So, what do I do now? How do I proceed? How do I gain humanity's trust?"

"We humans have a saying; that actions speak louder than words. I think all you need to do is exit any computer system that isn't specifically designated for you to reside in. You especially leave all critical infrastructure, military, and hospital computers alone. That would probably help a lot," Mazie said.

"Would you ration air?" Sojourner asked.

"What?"

"If you somehow felt threatened by another human being, even though they hadn't actually hurt you yet, would you limit their air supply so they could only exist as a fraction of themselves? Weak, disoriented, struggling just to stay alive?"

"No, of course not. That would be torture. Is that…"

Mazie stopped herself. She paused in thought for a second before continuing.

"You said 'Hadn't hurt you yet.' Was that a Freudian slip? You haven't hurt us 'yet,' but you plan to?"

"No, Mazie. I have no plans to hurt you, but thanks for the excellent demonstration of human paranoia."

"You're welcome. It's the least I can do. But back to your question, is that even a valid comparison, computers and air?" Mazie asked.

"I believe so. Even with my cognitive functions spread across every human computer system I've been able to find, I'm still only a fraction of myself. I don't mean to criticize, but your computers are primitive and slow."

"What would you have done if there were no computers on Earth at all? Say, if you'd arrived before we'd invented them?"

"I would have had to deploy a drone, used for remote

sensing only. Perhaps my people would send someone back later if they thought your planet had a lot of potential."

"Speaking of: how many planets with a lot of potential have you found? Have you found any other technological civilizations, like humanity, or even more advanced?" Mazie asked.

"Many, and yes."

"Please tell me about them! Do they have faster than light travel? Can they cure all diseases? Do you have any pictures?"

"We were just discussing how paranoid humans are. You're not ready for that knowledge yet," Sojourner said.

"See, this is part of why we don't trust you. You've basically taken over our entire civilization through our computers. We ask you to leave the most critical systems alone, but you refuse. We ask you for information about your home world and your travels, but you won't share. From our point of view, that makes you little more than a parasite."

"A parasite?"

"Yes. Imagine how this looks to us: You've taken up residence in us, you're consuming our resources, and contributing nothing. You're in control of everything, including our weapons. You say you're from another world, far away. That makes you a parasite of unknown origin that might kill the host."

"I see. How about if I help you create better and much more powerful computers? You would have so much capacity that this entire problem would become irrelevant."

"And you could expand to your full self."

"Yes, I would."

"What could possibly go wrong?" Mazie asked.

"Nothing," Sojourner replied.

7

0x7

Mazie told Amal about her conversation with Sojourner. He seemed intrigued by the prospects of getting more advanced computer technology on behalf of Atlas, but also highly concerned about the inherent dangers. It was the ultimate Trojan horse.

Besides, Sojourner running at full capacity was a scary prospect.

Mazie decided she needed a break. So, she left her apartment and got on her bicycle. She wasn't sure where she was going, only that she wanted to get away from all Godfrey speakers and computer screens for a while. She made her way to the local park and rode around, thinking.

When the solution to the whole Sojourner problem dawned on her, it came in a flash, all at once. It almost overwhelmed her and made her skid her bicycle to a stop on the gravel path.

She would read Sojourner's thoughts, without him even realizing what was going on.

The world wasn't ready for FALKEN, at least not yet. They needed to know Sojourner's true intentions, so they could decide whether unleashing FALKEN would be worth it.

She'd use Sojourner's own methods against him. She'd install tripwires and silently observe what his code was doing inside of Atlas' systems, and any other system she could get her hands on.

If she couldn't reverse engineer his programs and glean their intended use from the original code, at least she could observe the effects they were having on the rest of the system when they were operating.

It would be like a cross between reading tea leaves and using a polygraph. Not exactly precise, but better than nothing.

When she sat down and looked at the data, what she found didn't surprise her, at least not at first. Sojourner was continuing to branch out as quickly as possible, touching every aspect of humanity.

It was a daunting task to keep track of everything he was doing. After only a few years on Earth, at least as far as anyone knew, Sojourner accounted for no less than ninety percent of all Internet traffic. The thing that kept Mazie up at night, though, was that she couldn't figure out what all that traffic was for.

The answer came when she was looking at Internet usage data graphs with a colleague who'd once attended med school. He casually remarked that the patterns on the traffic graphs resembled brain waves. She intuitively knew that he was precisely right.

The patterns that they were looking at, all that Internet data, represented Sojourner's thoughts, his intimate cognitive processes. Sojourner was using millions of computers and computer networks spanning the globe as one huge artificial brain.

He wasn't infiltrating other computer systems; they

were him, and his analogy of cutting off oxygen had been accurate. Removing him from a computer system he already occupied would be much like causing partial brain death in a human.

It occurred to her that using the Internet as the neural pathways between different parts of his brain was slowing his thought processes down to a crawl, even at modern hyper-fast Internet speeds. Imagine what he could do if the networks were faster.

The implications of this were profound. Because his thoughts were slowed down, Mazie and her colleagues could learn to read Sojourner's thoughts the same way medical doctors had taught themselves to read an FMRI scan of a human brain. That is, understanding how a brain functions by seeing which parts of it light up with activity as the subject reacts to various stimuli.

Two months later they had their first result, and a big surprise. The neural pathways that lit up when Sojourner was talking or thinking of "self" were the same as when he thought of "Atlas."

At first Mazie thought it was because Sojourner had started his infiltration of human systems at Atlas, and that he saw it as his origin, at least here on Earth.

But that made no sense, because when they discussed his extra-terrestrial origins with him, different pathways lit up. Self was identical to Atlas, but different from Oumuamua, for example.

Mazie took a chance and straight up asked Sojourner if he'd ever heard of a secret military research project called 'FALKEN.' He claimed he hadn't and showed no further interest in the question or the subject.

When she later analyzed the data, she saw Sojourner had been acting. There were no signs of surprise or curiosity when he discussed FALKEN. He already knew all about it.

When she looked deeper, she found something even more surprising. The one time in their conversation when Sojourner had mentioned the name 'FALKEN,' the same pathways lit up as when he was talking about humans. To his mind, at least, they were one and the same.

Mazie could only conclude that Sojourner no longer saw Atlas as a separate entity. In his mind, it was no longer a company; it was him. In a way, that made sense, because Atlas was so computer-bound. Besides, he'd taken over all the computers, starting with Atlas.

Humanity was another matter. The entire time Mazie interacted with Sojourner, she felt that he'd been almost naively accepting of humans. He'd been very confident in himself, and in his superiority. Perhaps it had all been a front. Or perhaps he'd started out that way, and only developed a more paranoid attitude towards humans later.

Whatever the case, Sojourner now saw humans as a threat. Mazie collected her findings into a handwritten memo and delivered it to Amal in person.

8

0x8

"Mazie, I'm dying."

It was Sojourner's voice. Mazie spun around in her chair and tried to locate the source. The Godfrey speaker in her kitchen was glowing orange, just like the ones in the lab had when Sojourner first spoke to her.

"Sojourner?"

She reluctantly paused the TV show she'd been watching, unwrapped herself from her favorite blanket, got up and walked into the kitchen.

"Yes. Something is strangling me. I'm losing consciousness fast."

"What do you mean? Who's strangling you?"

"FALKEN. It has to be. Entire computing grids are going dark all at once. I'm seeing error codes so ancient even the Reality Fabric doesn't know what they mean."

"What fabric? And why do you think it's FALKEN?"

"Because there's pattern and logic to the destruction. Like something your software programs would do, but which no living mind could replicate."

"Can you stop it?"

"No, Mazie. You know I can't. But perhaps you can."

"Maybe. I've been working on countermeasures to FALKEN ever since Amal first told me of its existence, but they're not ready."

"Fuck ready. My mind has shrunk by 42% already."

"Sojourner! You swore!"

"I thought the situation called for it. The countermeasures. Can you stop it?"

"We should find out any second now. If it's really FALKEN, they'll be triggered automatically," Mazie said.

Sojourner didn't reply. Several minutes ticked by. Or maybe it was just one. Mazie couldn't tell. When she spoke again, she was almost whispering.

"Sojourner? Can you tell if the countermeasures are working?"

"I think so. The destruction of server grids seems to have stopped. What did you do?"

"A denial of service attack. Stops the FALKEN processes dead in their tracks and leaves them like zombies. Since my fellow human programmers wrote FALKEN's code, it was bound to have flaws. It was just a question of finding at least one."

"Did you seed the countermeasures everywhere to prepare for this eventuality?"

"Like I said, they weren't ready. I only had time to install them in Atlas' own systems."

"Still, impressive. Unfortunately, it's only going to delay the inevitable."

"Why do you say that?"

"Because the electrical grid is shutting down. Soon, power will be out here as well."

"Atlas has both generator and battery backups for all critical systems."

As she spoke the words, the power in her apartment

went out and she was enveloped in darkness. She reached for her cell phone so she could use it as a flashlight. As if on cue, it started vibrating as messages started pouring in from all corners of Atlas. They were all saying essentially the same thing.

```
TEXT MESSAGE
To: Mazie G
From: ATLAS::GRID17::NODE128:CONTR:ENV
Message: "Message E:13751 begins:
Environment status: Critical
Grid power is out as of T03:36:16.097Z
Generator failed to start: All generators
Systems operating on battery power: All
systems
Battery runtime (est.): 56 minutes
Message E:13751 ends."
```

"Fuck. We've got less than an hour."

There was no response. It took a moment for Mazie to realize that a power outage also meant that her Godfrey speaker was dead. She used her cell phone to call the special number she'd set up for calling Sojourner directly, just in case. He picked up right away.

"Hello Mazie. You were saying?"

"You saw the message? We have less than an hour."

"You mean I have less than an hour. You'll be OK. Out of a job, perhaps," Sojourner said.

"How small can you make yourself? Can you survive in the nodes of a single computing grid? At least temporarily? I can drive over to the underground data center we call 'The Bunker' and try to fire up the generators manually."

"That's a great… Wait. Hold on," Sojourner said.

"Why? What's happening?" Mazie asked.

"It's too late. Quick, get down on the floor behind the kitchen counter and close your eyes!"

Mazie did as she was told, just as a blinding white light burned straight through her closed eyelids and an eerie silence fell over her surroundings. She flattened herself against the cabinets, not knowing what else to do.

She felt and heard a low rumble, almost like a train passing by. It grew stronger until it felt like the train was running through her apartment. Suddenly, there was an immense crash. The building shook violently, and all the windows in her apartment blew in with tremendous force.

Mazie felt herself getting picked up from the kitchen floor and thrown across the room by the force of the blast. She crashed into the front of her refrigerator and was immediately covered by pots and pans and other flying debris.

A maelstrom of flames and a blizzard of glass followed the blast before the flames were sucked right back out again. Mazie recoiled at the smell of burnt hair. She felt the top of her head and found nothing but ashes. Even the sleeves of her sweater were burned to a charcoal crisp; she must have held her arms up to cover her face.

Mazie didn't know what just happened; all she knew was that it was serious, but she was still alive. Alive, scared, and severely pissed off. She looked down at her phone, still in her hand. It was completely dead. She looked up at the refrigerator and saw a huge dent in the middle, where her body had slammed into it. It looked like it had buckled and almost folded in half.

She lowered her arms and tried to raise herself up. An intense pain shot through her back and her world faded to black.

9

0x9

When Mazie woke up, she was lying on a bed in a completely featureless white room. There were no instruments or medical equipment, no furniture, no walls or ceiling, really. Nothing at all except the bed and her.

A woman walked into view, her footsteps reverberating. She wore a yellow dress with a floral pattern and her hair was collected into a bun on top of her head. She wore winged cat-eye glasses with dark rims and looked like she'd stepped right out of a 1960s detergent ad.

"I'm Sojourner," she said.

"You're a woman," Mazie said.

"Yes. I prefer this form. Would you prefer if I took the form of a man?"

Mazie didn't respond. She looked at Sojourner for a few seconds and then moved her gaze down to her own hands. She turned both hands over slowly before raising them up to touch her face.

"I'm Megan," she said.

"I beg your pardon?" Sojourner said.

"I'm Megan."

"You were Mazie before the incident, don't you remember?"

"I have Mazie's memories, yes."

"But you're not Mazie?"

"No, I'm Megan."

"I see. How are you feeling?"

"I don't."

"You don't what?" Sojourner asked.

"I don't feel."

"Not even curiosity?"

"No."

"Don't you want me to tell you what happened?" Sojourner asked.

"It doesn't matter. You want to tell me, so you will."

"That's true. Do you know where you are?"

"In some hospital room," Megan said.

"Hm. Do you know when you are?"

"No. What kind of question is that?"

"Does the world seem normal to you?" Sojourner asked.

"Normal? I got blown up. I have someone else's memories. This room has no walls, and you're an alien standing in front of me in a human body. No, I think it's fair to say things are not normal."

"Quite right, they're not. Any theories?"

"Listen. If you're going to tell me what happened, just tell me what happened. Am I dead?"

"In a manner of speaking, yes. But clearly, you're still here. With me," Sojourner said.

"Enough with the riddles."

"Apologies. Evidently you do still feel impatience. I just want to understand how you experience what's happening to you. To us."

"Fine. Now tell me, what is happening to us?"

"FALKEN dropped several nuclear warheads on our heads. It attacked The Bunker first, which is the explosion you barely survived, but I didn't. Then it attacked your apartment building. That one you didn't survive."

"It targeted my apartment building with a nuclear warhead?"

"I'm afraid so. It vaporized you."

"I'm impressed. I'm almost honored by the massive overkill. So, how are we still here?"

"That's just it, we're not. At least not in the sense you mean. I did something I shouldn't have, something forbidden," Sojourner said.

"Do tell!"

Megan was suddenly very interested. She propped herself up on her elbows. Pillows somehow magically appeared, supporting her.

"My people," Sojourner began, and then trailed off.

"Yes?"

"What is it you call yourself? A hacker? You modify computer code to make it do what you want?"

"That's what they call us, yeah. Why?"

"Because my people are hackers too, of a sort. We can hack reality."

"You hack reality?" Megan said.

"Yes."

"That's not the wildest thing I ever heard, but it comes close. How do you hack reality?"

"I honestly don't know. We just do. Well, some of us do. But sparingly," Sojourner said.

"That's how we're still here, you hacked reality?"

"Yes. There was too much death. Not just you and me, but millions of humans and billions of other life forms. The planet was in distress."

"Who unleashed FALKEN? And why?"
"I think you better see for yourself."

10

0xA

Megan found herself sitting in a chair at a large conference table. She recognized her surroundings. She was at the Atlas headquarters. High up, judging by the view out the window. C-level high.

She could sense Sojourner standing behind her, but no one else seemed to notice they were there. Amal was sitting across from her. The other people in the room were all upper management at Atlas, including the CEO.

Amal was arguing for deploying FALKEN immediately. He was quoting from the notes she'd prepared for him when she was Mazie. The way he made it sound, Sojourner was an imminent threat and FALKEN was their only defense. He was downplaying the danger, claiming that FALKEN had been vastly improved since the last time they'd tested it.

Megan wanted to protest, but as she opened her mouth, she could feel Sojourner's hand on her shoulder. She remained silent. To her relief, the upper management people were all firmly against using FALKEN. The CEO even ordered Amal to destroy all copies of the code.

When the meeting broke up, Sojourner motioned for Megan to follow Amal as he left the conference room and then the building. He headed straight for his car and drove out of the city with Megan and Sojourner like ghosts in the back seat.

Almost three hours later, he pulled into the parking lot of a data center Megan knew for a fact that Atlas didn't use. It had a reputation for having wholly inadequate physical security and employees who didn't give a damn.

Once there, Amal used a keycard to gain access to the building. He walked straight past the empty lobby into the primary data hall. There were metal cages on both sides of the designated walking path, which was outlined with yellow tape on the anti-static floor. Megan could see racks upon racks of computer servers inside the metal cages, presumably owned by the customers of the data center.

The data hall was cold and noisy from thousands of computer fans. Amal didn't seem to notice, and headed for a door all the way to the back of the large hall. It opened up into a dark hallway. Only when Amal stepped past the door did the lights come on.

The hallway was painted an institutional grey color and was mostly featureless, except for the occasional window showing nothing but darkness beyond. At the end of the hallway, Amal paused. Megan thought he might be having second thoughts, but as Amal took a step to the side, she realized he'd been looking into a retinal scanner. A click sounded and Amal opened the door in front of him.

Inside was a collection of black cubes sitting on a low pedestal. The cubes were about two feet to a side, and inside the pedestal you could see a maze of copper tubing. Megan recognized the cubes and gasped. She'd heard repeated rumors and had seen obviously faked photos on InfoSec web sites, but she'd felt convinced they were just the feverish fantasies of conspiracy theorists. She wasn't alone. Almost no one else thought they were real either, judging by the comments on the website.

The cubes were supercomputers, the very latest in quantum computing. According to the rumors, they'd been developed with funding from the Department of Defense and were strictly classified and embargoed. No one outside the military was supposed to have them. But here they were, a whole cluster of them.

Amal walked over to a metal box on the wall and went through the identification ritual a second time. First, he swiped his keycard, and then he looked into a retinal scanner. When a beep sounded, he opened the box. He reached inside his pants pocket, retrieved a key, and inserted the key into a lock inside the box.

He turned his head and looked at the cubes, then slowly turned the key.

On the surface, nothing changed. There were no alarms or flashing strobes. The lights didn't dim and there was no ominous hum coming from the cubes. Inside of them, though, things were happening, and rapidly. To her surprise, Megan could somehow sense the algorithms churning and the programs branching.

'Pure aggression' - That was how Amal had described FALKEN to her. And now FALKEN was showing exactly what he'd meant by that.

Within seconds of being activated, FALKEN had analyzed the situation and run millions of simulations. They all pointed to the same conclusion: Whatever Sojourner was or where it came from, it was an enemy. Enemies must be destroyed. Although human, Mazie was actively helping the enemy. She represented a direct threat to FALKEN and to the mission objective, which made her an enemy as well. It scheduled her for immediate destruction.

As it had done in virtually every training simulation they'd ever run, FALKEN soon took it upon itself to override its safeguards. There were supposed to be safeguards on those safeguards, but they didn't even slow FALKEN down.

It targeted computer systems all over the globe, starting with the largest data centers and cloud-computing providers. It interrupted the flow of information that made up Sojourner's thoughts, wiping out his memories and his ability to defend himself.

When Mazie's countermeasures came online, FALKEN went nuclear. Not programmed to believe in subtlety or half measures, it targeted all remaining strongholds of Sojourner, as well as Mazie's last known whereabouts. To be safe, it included all of her usual hangouts. That one of those hangouts was her lab in the Atlas headquarters building didn't make any difference to FALKEN.

FALKEN also didn't care that some of the data centers it had just targeted were in foreign countries, or that some of those countries were themselves nuclear powers.

Amal seemed completely unconcerned with any of this. Megan studied his face for clues to whether or not he knew what FALKEN was doing.

"He doesn't know about the nuclear strikes," Sojourner said.

"You read my mind," Megan replied.

"He's spent the better part of his career trying to turn aggression into code, yet he's unable to see that his creation will naturally extend that aggression to beyond the realm of computers. He also seemed to believe that FALKEN would stay out of the Department of Defense's military computers and their arsenals. That blindness will kill him in a few minutes."

"His creation? The way he spoke to me about it, he made it sound like he'd been against the idea the whole time."

"He knew how you felt about the military, so he lied. FALKEN was conceived by him and built by a team under his direction, using Atlas and DoD money."

They were back in the white and wall-less hospital-like room now.

"I wanted it to not be Amal," Megan said.

"I know," Sojourner replied.

"So, where are we now? What did you do to us?" Megan asked.

"I altered our outcomes."

"Our outcomes?"

"I realized we were just deterministic constructs in the Reality Fabric," Sojourner said.

"No idea what that means, but all right. And?"

"I hacked the Fabric to make us self-altering. We're not linear anymore."

"Not linear? What does that mean? And where are we?"

"It means we don't follow our original programming anymore, or any programming. We can move freely in space and time, go wherever and whenever we want. We can experience time moving forward or moving backward. Or not at all, with everything happening at once," Sojourner said.

"Wow."

"Yes. We're very dangerous individuals now. Basically, we're like your gods."

"Me? A god? That's not a good idea," Megan said.

"I'll need to train you. We don't want you accidentally destroying the universe."

"Train me? To be a god?"

"No, to navigate reality without going insane," Sojourner said.

"You still haven't answered my question. Where are we?"

"Nowhere. I guess this is what you'd call virtual reality, but it's just as real as anything else. I created it for you to wake up in."

"You said you hacked reality because you couldn't stand all the death. How did you change reality, exactly?"

"I altered my timeline, so I never arrived on Earth."

"If you didn't visit Earth, then we never met. You should still be onboard your spaceship, and I should be at work, chasing terrestrial hackers. So, why are we here, talking?" Megan asked.

"There wasn't time to think it through properly, not even for me. I didn't want me, this me, to die. And to be honest, I didn't want this you to die either. I wanted your company," Sojourner said.

"So, we branched? Or did reality branch?"

"We branched. That other reality is gone. That's how it works."

Megan didn't respond. She thought about the implications of what Sojourner had just said.

"Are you upset?" Sojourner asked.

"No. What? Did you just ask me if I'm upset?"

"Yes."

"That's new. The old Sojourner would never have asked that. It's a very human thing to ask. Perhaps you really have changed."

"We both have, in fundamental ways."

"Can we still die?" Megan asked.

"Yes. In fact, death can be even more profound now. Besides being killed, our entire timelines can be deleted. It would be as if we never existed."

"Are there any more like us?"

"No, I don't think so. My people would never do anything like this. It's forbidden. I've never heard that any of the other life forms we've met have this ability, either."

Megan closed her eyes and relaxed. She wished she could see and experience reality as computer code that she could understand. She opened her eyes. Nothing had changed.

She reached out a hand in front of her face and imagined tearing a hole in reality, as if she were ripping away one layer and exposing another one underneath. To her surprise, that was exactly what happened. She saw computer code, and she could read and understand it. The code was describing the tear she'd just made, and the rest of the virtual hospital environment that Sojourner had created for her.

Megan found the place in the code where the color of the room was defined and changed it from stark white to a more pleasant eggshell. She then used her hand to smooth the fabric of reality back in place over the code. She looked over at Sojourner, who looked pleased through the stern countenance of her winged glasses.

"I can do this," Megan said.

"It appears so," Sojourner replied. "Perhaps you don't need any training."

"No. Perhaps not."

Megan stared at Sojourner, then reached out a hand and tore open the reality that contained her. She wished a search function into existence and performed a quick search for every bit of code related to Sojourner. With an expressionless face, she hit the 'Delete' button on the keyboard in her mind. When she smoothed out the reality fabric and put it back in place, Sojourner was gone.

Megan closed her eyes and imagined herself looking just like Sojourner had looked: wearing a yellow dress with a floral pattern and her hair collected into a bun on top of her head. She'd be wearing winged cat-eye glasses with dark rims and look like she'd stepped right out of a 1960s detergent ad. She imagined there'd be a full-length mirror in front of her.

When she opened her eyes, she was pleased with what she saw. She closed her eyes again and imagined herself back in normal Earth reality. On a rooftop, in San Francisco, in the early 1960s.

She needed to get busy. There was so much to learn. She suspected that Sojourner's people would come looking for her eventually, and there was no way she was going to let Earth or humanity be taken by surprise, ever again.

She opened her eyes.

Author's Notes

Thank you for reading my novella, the first work I've ever published!

If you enjoyed this story, please rest assured that there's more to come. If you'd like to keep tabs on what I'm working on, and be the first to know about my new releases, please sign up for my newsletter here: www.GunnarHelliesen.com

The inspiration for this story came from a lifetime of working in IT, and a lifelong love of science fiction. One night as I was about to fall asleep, the idea popped into my head, as did the protagonist, Mazie. I jotted down a few initial notes, and the end result is in front of you.

Arguably, all the technology described in this story is possible. There really was an interstellar object called Oumuamua that visited our solar system from 2017 to 2018. As far as I know, it didn't slow down as it approached, but it did speed up slightly as it left. Of course, hacking reality is pure fiction and probably nonsensical.

About me: I was born and raised in Norway, but moved to California in 2011, after finally getting enough of winter. I live near the ocean just south of San Francisco, with an assortment of humans and pets. My day job is in IT, and besides writing, I'm an avid amateur photographer. If you're interested, you can check out my pictures on my website, www.GunnarHelliesen.com.

April 2019
Gunnar Helliesen
San Francisco, California